To my friend.

Blaze

Gary Harbo
2008

Where Is My Sister?

Written and Illustrated by
Gary Harbo

Where is My Sister?

Written and Illustrated by
Gary Harbo

Published by KUTIE KARI BOOKS, INC.

Printed in the United States of America

To order books visit Gary's website:
www.garyharbo.com

or write to:

Kutie Kari Books
4189 Ethan Drive
Eagan, MN 55123

ISBN 1-884149-40-5

Dedicated to

Gavin and Grant

You keep me young in heart

and young in mind...

Thank you Lord for blessing me so greatly!

I looked over here.

Then I looked over there!

I could not find her.

"Does anyone care?"

She's not in the bushes,

not in the trees.

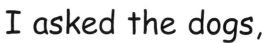

I asked the dogs,

and even their fleas!

I raced to the lion's cage,

praying on the way.

But, if they knew

where she was at

they would not say.

"Where is my sister?"

I screamed to the birds.

They gave me a look,

but not a word.

5

I ran to the bear's den,

and pleaded for help.

She scratched my head.

I let out a yelp!

6

"What does she look like?"

asked the pig in a pen

"What does she look like?"

he asked me again!

7

"She's tall and thin,

like a long string bean.

Her hair is a mess,

if you know what I mean."

"I think I saw her,"

said the monkey up high.

"But I"ll only tell you,

when that pig can fly!"

I started to get mad,

it wasn't a joke.

My voice was trembling,

when finally I spoke.

"Where is my sister?"

I demanded to know.

My eyes were like fire,

I was ready to blow...

"Settle down!",

Said a fish in the tank.

"I saw her at the pond,

laying down by the bank."

I raced for the pond,

as fast as I could run.

I saw a turtle that was sleeping,

on a rock in the sun.

13

When I reached the pond,

and raced for the shore.

I saw a snake

and a gator,

but nothing more...

I must find my sister.

What should I do?

"Where is my sister?"

I cried to the two.

The snake looked,

and gave me a wink.

"I'll tell you where she is,

and it's not where you think."

"The gator ate her"

he said with a grin.

"The gator ate her"

he hissed it again!

17

"The gator ate her?"

I screamed in reply.

"That can't be the truth.

It must be a lie!"

"Why would I lie?

What good would it do?

Look at the gator,

is that her old shoe?"

I looked at the gator,

and much to my shock.

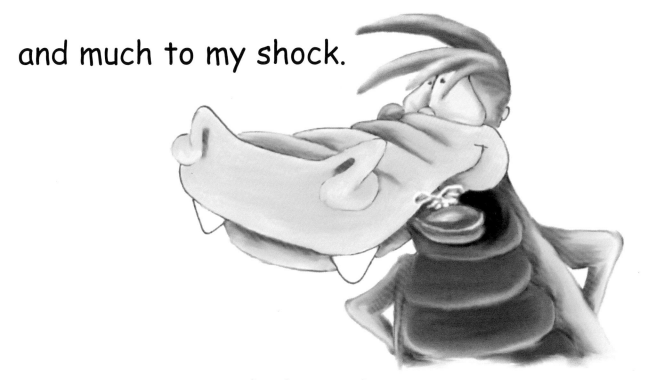

It was not only her shoe,

but also her sock!

I jumped on the gator

and grabbed his big snout.

I pulled it wide open,

but she didn't come out!

The gator was worried.

There was fear in his eyes.

I didn't know if I could save her,

but I had to try....

I rolled him on his back,

and it wasn't easy to do.

He grunted and groaned

and spit out her shoe.

The monkeys raced over,

to see the action unfold.

They swung from the trees,

and watched from the road.

24

The elephants came running,

when they heard of a fight.

They stopped in their tracks,

when they came within sight.

The giraffes kept their distance,

because they could see over the crowd.

But even in the distance,

it was getting very loud.

The bears came quickly,

and climbed up a tree.

They heard the excitement,
and wanted to see.

27

The gorilla beat his chest,

as I grabbed the gators tail.

"Let go of my sister,

or over the tree you will sail."

28

"I did not eat your sister,

that I wouldn't do.

All I wanted to eat,

was her sock and her shoe."

"Then where is my sister?

I just have to know.

I can see her socks,

but where are her toes?"

"Here I am brother!"

as I heard her bare feet.

"The gator and I

were hungry,

so I got us something to eat!"

"Can you forgive me?"

I said to my zoo friend.

"I jumped to a conclusion,

it won't happen again!"

The End